THESE ARE THE X-MEN

By Thomas Macri

Illustrated by Ramon Bachs *and* Hi-Fi Design

Based on the Marvel comic book series The X-Men

New York
Los Angeles

marvelkids.com

© 2013 MARVEL

Published by Marvel Press, an imprint of Disney Book Group. No part of this book may be reproduced or transmitted in any form or by any means, electronic or mechanical, including photocopying, recording, or by any information storage and retrieval system, without written permission from the publisher. For information address Marvel Press, 1101 Flower Street, Glendale, California 91201.

Printed in the United States of America
First Edition
1 3 5 7 9 10 8 6 4 2
G658-7729-4-12061
ISBN 978-1-4231-7083-9

These are the X-Men.

Professor X leads the X-Men.
He can read minds.

He cannot move his legs.
He stays in his wheelchair.

The X-Men train in
a special gym.

It is called the
Danger Room.
It can look like anything.

The X-Men are a team.
They work together.

Many heroes are X-Men.

The X-Men are mutants.
Mutants are born with powers.

These are a few X-Men.

This is Wolverine.
He is an X-Man.

He has claws.

His claws can cut metal.

This is Cyclops.
His eyes shoot blasts.

His blasts can
stop anything.
They can even stop
big robots!

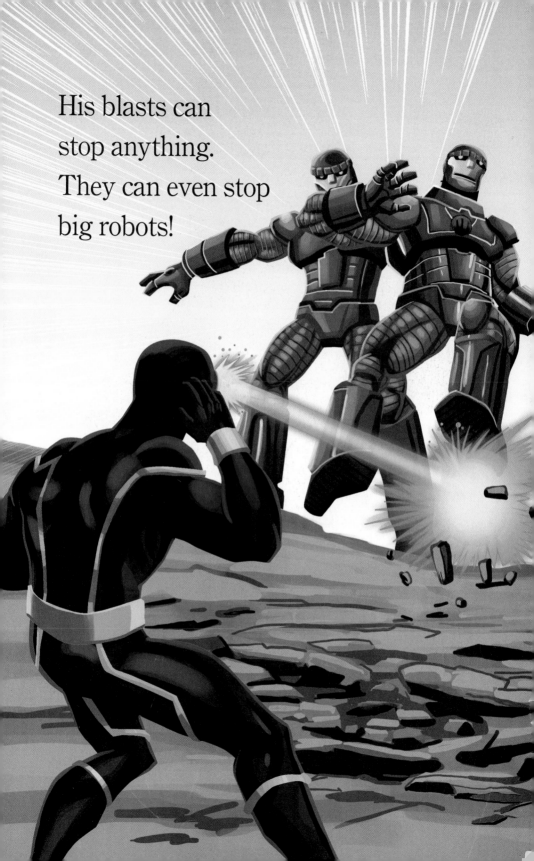

Cyclops has a brother.
His name is Havok.
He is an X-Man, too.

He can shoot power
from his hands.

Storm can make thunder.
She can make lightning.
She can make it rain.

She can fly on the wind.

This is Nightcrawler.
He can hide in
dark places.

He can move in a puff
of smoke.

This is Kitty Pryde.

Kitty can walk
through walls.

Colossus is an X-Man.
He can turn to metal.
He can smash bricks!

Banshee is an X-Man, too.

His scream is loud.
It is very powerful.

This is Polaris.

Polaris can move metal.
She can even bend it.

Beast is an X-Man.
He can jump high.
Angel has wings.
He can fly.

Iceman is an X-Man, too.
He can turn to ice.
He can freeze things.

Marvel Girl uses her mind
to move things.

She can even move
a truck!

Some X-Men can fly.

Some X-Men cannot.

But all X-Men are
Super Heroes.
These are the X-Men.